Richard Scarry's
Funniest
Storybook
Ever

First published in Great Britain in 1972.
This edition published by HarperCollins Children's Books in 2011.

HarperCollins Children's Books is a division of HarperCollins Publishers Ltd,
77-85 Fulham Palace Road, London W6 8JB

1 3 5 7 9 10 8 6 4 2

ISBN: 978-0-00-793522-2

The HarperCollins website address is www.harpercollins.co.uk

Printed and bound in China.

Richard Scarry's
Funniest Storybook Ever

HarperCollins *Children's Books*

The Talking Bread

Humperdink, the baker, was mixing bread dough with the help of Able Baker Charlie Mouse. His little girl, Flossie, watched them squish and squash the dough.

After they had kneaded the dough by squishing and squashing, they patted it into loaves of all different shapes and sizes.

Then Humperdink put the uncooked loaves of bread into the hot oven to bake.

After the loaves had finished baking, Humperdink set them out
on the table to cool. M-m-m-m-m! Fresh bread smells good!

Mamma!

Finally he took out the last loaf.
LISTEN! Did you hear that?
When he picked up the loaf, it said,
"Mamma." But everybody knows that
bread can't talk.
IT MUST BE HAUNTED!!!

"HELP! POLICE!"
Humperdink picked up Flossie and ran from the room.
"I must telephone Sergeant Murphy," he said.

Sergeant Murphy arrived in a hurry.

He reached down and picked up
the loaf of haunted bread.

"Mamma!" the bread said.

Mamma!

Murphy was so startled that he
fell into the mixing trough.

Just at that moment, Huckle and
Lowly came into the bakery.

"That is a very strange loaf of bread," said Lowly.
Stretching out, he slowly ooched across the floor towards it.

He took a nibble. The bread said nothing.

He nibbled and nibbled into the loaf until only his foot was showing… and still the bread said nothing.

Mamma!

Lowly stood up. The bread said, "Mamma!"
Lowly took another nibble, then stuck out his head. "I have solved the mystery," he said. "Break the loaf open very gently, but please… don't break me!"

Humperdink gently broke open the bread and inside was…Flossie's DOLL!
It had fallen into the mixing trough and had been baked inside the bread.

With the mystery solved, they all sat down to eat the haunted bread. All of them, that is, except Lowly. He had already eaten his fill.

Mamma!

Baby!

All right, Lowly! Please take your foot off the table!

Absent-Minded
Mr. Rabbit

Mr. Rabbit walked down the street. He wasn't looking at the workmen, who were making a new, hot, sticky, gooey street. No! He was looking at his newspaper.

He wasn't looking at his feet, which were getting hot and sticky and gooey, too. No! He was looking at his newspaper.

Then suddenly he stopped looking at his newspaper. He looked down at his feet instead. And do you know what he saw? He saw that he was STUCK in that hot, sticky, gooey street!

The workmen got a long pole and tried to poke him out. It didn't work.

A truck tried to pull him out with a rope. No good! He was stuck all right!

They tried to blow him out with a huge fan. The fan blew off his hat and coat…
but Mr. Rabbit remained stuck.

Some firemen tried to squirt him out. They squirted off his shirt
and tie – but Mr. Rabbit remained stuck. REALLY STUCK!
Well, now! He can't stay there forever! Somebody has
to think of a way to get him out.

Aha! Here comes a power shovel!
Let's see what it will try to do.

Well, the power shovel reached down… and scooped up Mr. Rabbit.

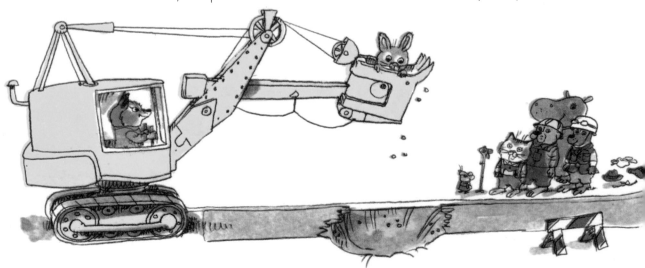

It dropped him gently to the dry ground. He would certainly have to wash his feet when he got home, but at least he was no longer stuck.

He put on his clothes and thanked everyone.
As he was leaving, he promised that after this
he would always look where he was going.

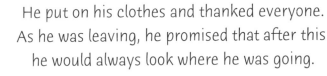

But a little while later he was reading his newspaper again. He had forgotten his promise. And, naturally, he wasn't watching where he was going.

OH!!! DON'T LOOK!!!!

Sergeant Murphy and the Banana Thief

Sergeant Murphy was busy putting parking tickets on cars when, suddenly, who should come running out of the market but Bananas Gorilla. He had stolen a bunch of bananas, and was trying to escape.

Murphy! LOOK! He is stealing your motorcycle, too!

Sergeant Murphy was furious. Huckle and Lowly Worm were watching. Huckle said, "You may borrow my tricycle to chase after him if you want to."

B-r-e-e-e-t!

Away they went… chasing after that naughty thief.

They raced through the crowded streets. Don't YOU ever ride your tricycle in the street!

They crossed a drawbridge just as it was
opening to let a boat go through.

Bananas stopped suddenly and went into a restaurant.

Murphy said to Louie, who was the owner, "I am looking for a thief!"
Together, they searched the whole restaurant, but they couldn't find
Bananas anywhere.
Louie then said, "Sit down and relax, Murphy. I will bring you and
your friends something delicious to eat."

Somebody had better pick up those banana skins before someone slips on one.
Don't you think so?

Louie brought them a bowl of banana soup. Lowly said, "I'll bet Bananas Gorilla would like to be here right now."

"Huckle, we mustn't forget to wash our hands before eating," said Sergeant Murphy. So off they went to wash. Lowly went along, too.

When they came back, they discovered that their table had disappeared.

Indeed, it was slowly creeping away… when it slipped on a banana skin! And guess who was hiding underneath.

Sergeant Murphy, we are very proud of you! Bananas must be punished. Some day he has to learn that it is naughty to steal things which belong to others.

Speedboat Spike

Speedboat Spike liked to take his little boy,
Swifty, out for a ride in his speedboat. Oh, my!
Didn't Spike think he was the greatest!

Once he rammed into a sailing boat.

Say! Why don't you look where you're going?

Another time he bumped into a barge and knocked a lady's washing overboard.
(Swifty! Why don't you tell your father to stop driving dangerously?)

Speedboat Spike just wouldn't slow down, and he wouldn't stop bumping into things.

STOP!

POLICE

But that was before Officer Barnacle caught him... and made him stop!

Officer Barnacle ordered Speedboat Spike to keep his speedboat in a paddling pool UP ON LAND! Now Spike can go as fast as he likes, but he won't be able to bump into anyone.

POLICE

But who is that I see in that tiny little speedboat? Why, it's his little boy, Swifty! Oh dear! I think we are going to need another paddling pool. Go get him, Officer Barnacle!

Ma Pig's New Car

Pa Pig bought a new car to give to Ma Pig on her birthday.
She will certainly be surprised when she sees her new car, won't she?

On the way home, Pa stopped at a store. When he came out, he got into a
jeep by mistake. (You should be wearing your glasses, Pa Pig!) Harry and Sally
thought that Pa had swapped cars with a soldier.

Then he went to the supermarket. When he came out he got into a police car.
"You made a good swap, Daddy," said Harry. But Pa wasn't listening… and he
didn't seem to be thinking very well either. Don't you agree?

Next he drove to a fruit stand to buy some apples. When he left he took Farmer Fox's tractor. My, but Pa is absent-minded, isn't he? "Ma will certainly like her new tractor," said Sally to Harry.

Then they stopped to watch a fire. When the fire was out they left – in the fire engine! How can *anyone* make so many mistakes?

Hey, Joe! You forgot to turn off the engine.

Then they stopped to watch some workers who were digging a big hole in the ground. No! Pa did NOT get into that dump truck. But by mistake, he got into...

…Roger Rhino's power shovel!
Ma Pig was certainly surprised to see her new CAR!
But, Pa! Do you know how to stop it?

Yes, he did!
Oh, oh! Here comes Roger now. He has found
Ma Pig's new car and is bringing it to her.
It looks as though he is very angry with that
someone who took his power shovel.

ROGER! PLEASE BE CAREFUL! You are squeezing Ma's little car
just a little bit too tightly. Well, let's all hope that Pa Pig will never
again make *that* many mistakes in one day!

The Three Fishermen

Lowly, Huckle, and Daddy were going fishing.

Their little motorboat took them far away from shore.

Daddy said, "Throw out the anchor, Lowly." Lowly threw the anchor out...and himself with it!

Lowly climbed back in and Daddy began to fish.

Daddy caught an old bicycle. But he didn't want an old bicycle. He wanted a fish.

Then Huckle fell overboard. Wouldn't you know that something like that would happen?

Daddy pulled Huckle out. Why, look there! Huckle has caught a fish in his pants!

Daddy fished some more, but he couldn't catch anything. He was disgusted. "Let's go home," he said. "There just aren't any fish down there."

As Daddy was getting out of the boat, he slipped... and fell! Oh, boy! Is he angry now!

But why is he yelling so loudly?

Aha! I see! A fish was biting his tail. The fish was trying to catch Daddy. It is good that Daddy has a strong tail. Now Lowly is the only one who hasn't caught…

Wow!

But look! Lowly has taken off his hat. Do you see what is under it? A FISH! Very good, Lowly.

Yes, there you see three very good fishermen!

The Accident

Harvey Pig was driving down the street.
(Better keep your eyes on the road, Harvey.)

Well! He didn't keep his eyes on the road and he had an accident.

B-r-e-e-e-t!

Sergeant Murphy came riding along. "Everyone get onto the pavement," he said. "I don't want anyone arguing in the street. You might get run over."
So everyone got onto the pavement.

And just in time, too! Rocky was driving his bulldozer down the street.
"I'm very sorry about that," he said. "I guess I wasn't looking where I was going."

All right, now. Keep calm, everybody!
Here comes Greasy George, the garage mechanic.

Greasy George towed away the cars, and the motorcycle, and all the loose pieces.
"I will fix everything just like new," he said. "Come and get them in about a week."

Greasy George worked and worked to make everything just like new again. Stand back, Lowly and Huckle! Don't get too close to him!

Well! Greasy George was certainly telling the truth. When everyone came back, everything was certainly NEW! I don't know how you did it, Greasy George, but I think you have the parts a little bit mixed up!

My cap!

Calling Sergeant Murphy! Your little girl, Bridget, won't take her nap. Hurry home immediately

Please Move to the Back of the Bus

Ollie was a bus driver. All day long he called out to his passengers,
"Please move to the back of the bus."

At every single bus stop, he would politely say, "Please move to the
back of the bus. There are others who want to get on."

Look! See how his bus is filling up!

But look there! The back of the bus is empty. No one will move back.
Ah! Here comes Big Hilda. *She* will move to the back of the bus.

Big Hilda just managed to squeeze
on. By this time Ollie was furious.
"I am not going to drive any farther,"
he shouted, "until everyone moves
to the back of the bus!"

Does this bus g

Oh, oh! Hilda *did* move to the back of the bus – and she moved everyone else with her!
Poor Ollie! Now he *couldn't* drive the bus any farther.
All right. Everybody out! This is the end of the line.

Uncle Willy and the Pirates

Not a soul dared to go sailing.
Do you know why? There was a wicked
band of pirates about, and they would
steal anything they could get their
hands on! But Uncle Willy wasn't afraid.
"They won't bother me," he said.

He dropped his anchor near a deserted island.
Aunty Pastry had baked him a pie for his lunch.
"I think I will have a little nap before I eat my pie,"
said Uncle Willy to himself.

Uncle Willy went to sleep. B-z-z-z-z-z.
What is THAT I see climbing on board? A PIRATE!
And another! And another? PIRATES, UNCLE WILLY!

But Uncle Willy couldn't do a thing.
There were just too many pirates.

First, they put Uncle Willy on the deserted island.
Then they started to eat his pie.
"M-m-m-m-m! DEE-licious!" they all said.

Uncle Willy was furious. He didn't care so
much about the pie, but he needed his boat if he
was ever going to get home again.
Then Uncle Willy had an idea. He gathered some
branches, some sea-shells, and some long beach grass.
He wove the beach grass into a kind of cloth.

Then he tied some sea-shells onto the branches and made a ferocious-looking mouth.

He tied the grass cloth onto the mouth, then attached some sea-shell eyes. By the time he tied on a spiky palm leaf, he had made a ferocious MONSTER!

Uncle Willy got inside. He was now "Uncle Willy, THE FEROCIOUS MONSTER." Look out, you pirates!

The Ferocious Monster swam out to the boat. The pirates were terrified.

They all ran into the cabin to hide.
The Ferocious Monster closed the door
behind them – and locked it.

The Monster had captured the wicked pira[tes]

Then the Monster sailed back home. Aunty Pastry
saw it from the dock. She was terrified!
"There is a horrible Monster coming!" she cried.
"He is even worse than the pirates!"

Uncle Willy landed, and took off his monst[er]
suit. Everyone said, "Thank goodness it wa[s]
only you!" Sergeant Murphy took the pirat[es]
away to be punished.

Well… Uncle Willy had made the seas safe
to sail on again. Hooray for Uncle Willy –
THE FEROCIOUS MONSTER!!!

How was the pie, Uncle Willy?

You BAD pie rats!!!

The Unlucky Day

Mr. Raccoon opened his eyes. "Wake up, Mamma," he said. "It looks like a good day."

He turned on the water. The tap broke off. "Call Mr. Fixit, Mamma," he said.

He sat down to breakfast. He burned his toast. Mamma burned his bacon.

Mamma told him to bring home food for supper. As he was leaving, the door fell off its hinges.

Driving down the road, Mr. Raccoon had a flat tyre.

While he was changing it, his trousers ripped.

He started again. His car engine exploded and wouldn't go any farther.

He decided to walk. The wind blew his hat away. Bye-bye, hat!

While chasing after his hat,
he fell into a manhole.

Then he climbed out and bumped
into a lamp post.

A policeman yelled at him for
bending the lamp post.

"I must be more careful," thought Mr. Raccoon.
"This is turning into a bad day."

He didn't look where he was going.
He bumped into Mrs. Rabbit and broke
all her eggs.

Another policeman gave him a ticket for
littering the pavement.

His friend Warty Warthog came up
behind him and patted him on the back.
Warty! Don't pat so hard!
"Come," said Warty. "Let's go to a
restaurant for lunch."

Warty ate and ate and ate. Have you ever seen such bad table manners? Take off your hat, Warty!

Warty finished and left without paying for what he had eaten. Mr. Raccoon had to pay for it. Just look at all the plates that Warty used!

The lunch cost Mr. Raccoon every penny he had with him. "What other bad things can happen to me today?" he wondered.

Well... for one thing, the tablecloth could catch on his belt buckle!

"Don't you ever come in here again!" the waiter shouted.

"I think I had better go home as quickly as possible," thought Mr. Raccoon. "I don't want to get into any more trouble."

He arrived home just as Mr. Fixit was leaving. Mr. Fixit had spent the entire day finding new leaks. "I will come back tomorrow to fix the leaks," said Mr. Fixit.

Mrs. Raccoon asked her husband if he had brought home the food she asked for. She wanted to cook something hot for supper. Of course Mr. Raccoon hadn't, so they had to eat cold pickles for supper.

After supper they went upstairs to bed. "There isn't another unlucky thing that can happen to me today," said Mr. Raccoon as he got into bed. Oh, dear! His bed broke! I do hope that Mr. Raccoon will have a better day tomorrow, don't you?

Lowly Worm's Birthday

It was Lowly's birthday.

Mother Cat was going to bake a birthday cake. Father was going to town to buy some eggs for the cake, and some candles to put on it. And maybe a few other things as well. "Be careful you don't break the eggs," said Mother.

Father Cat stopped at the hardware shop to buy some birthday candles. HE LEFT THE CAR ENGINE RUNNING!!! You know better than to do THAT, Father Cat!

Now! See what happened. The car drove off all by itself! I don't think Lowly knows how to drive. Anyway, he certainly doesn't have a driver's licence.

The car headed for the supermarket to get the eggs for Lowly's birthday cake. As it went past the egg counter, Lowly picked up some fresh eggs. Father Cat had to pay the cashier for them.

SOAP

SPECIAL TODAY! FRESH EGGS IN A BASKET

ickles

They drove out through the back door of the supermarket.

They passed Mr. Fixit, who was fixing a broken traffic light. Hurry up and fix it, Mr. Fixit, before there is a bad accident!

Don't be a litter lout!

Hang onto those eggs, Lowly… and don't break any!

But where is Father Cat? Oh! There he is! He has just bought some balloons and favours at the party shop.

Through Farmer Alfalfa's hayfield they went. I don't think Farmer Alfalfa liked that.
But then… it was the car's fault. No one was steering it.

Father Cat was still chasing after them. He stopped for a moment in order to
buy some of Mrs. Alfalfa's delicious fresh strawberries. He thought they would
look very nice on Lowly's birthday cake.

At last they all came to a stop in Mother Cat's kitchen!

My babies!
My Lowly!

Lowly hadn't broken a *single* egg!

Mother Cat baked a huge birthday cake, and guess who had the first bite! It was Lowly's most exciting birthday ever! Happy birthday, dear Lowly...Happy birthday to YOU!

Happy birthday, Lowly!

Mamma!

Baby!